THE MILKMAID
AND HER PAIL

Retold by BLAKE HOENA
Illustrations by ISABEL MUNOZ
Music by JOSEPH FAISON IV

CANTATA
LEARNING

WWW.CANTATALEARNING.COM

CANTATA LEARNING

Published by Cantata Learning
1710 Roe Crest Drive
North Mankato, MN 56003
www.cantatalearning.com

Library of Congress Cataloging-in-Publication Data
Names: Hoena, B. A., author. | Munoz, Isabel, illustrator. | Faison, Joseph, IV,
  composer. | Aesop.
Title: The milkmaid and her pail / retold by Blake Hoena ; illustrated by
  Isabel Munoz ; music by Joseph Faison IV.
Description: North Mankato, MN : Cantata Learning, [2018] | Series: Classic
  fables in rhythm and rhyme | Summary: A modern song retells the fable of a
  maiden whose daydreams of what she will buy with the money she expects to
  earn for a pail of milk she carries earn her a valuable lesson, instead.
  Includes a brief introduction to Aesop, sheet music, glossary, discussion
  questions, and further reading.
Identifiers: LCCN 2017017523 (print) | LCCN 2017035545 (ebook) | ISBN
  9781684101627 (ebook)| ISBN 9781684101238 (hardcover : alk. paper)
Subjects: | CYAC: Behavior--Songs and music. | Fables. | Folklore. | Songs.
Classification: LCC PZ8.3.H667 (ebook) | LCC PZ8.3.H667 Mil 2018 (print) |
  DDC 398.2 [E] --dc23
LC record available at https://lccn.loc.gov/2017017523

Book design and art direction, Tim Palin Creative
Editorial direction, Kellie M. Hultgren
Music direction, Elizabeth Draper
Music arranged and produced by Joseph Faison IV

Printed in the United States of America in North Mankato, Minnesota.
122017   0378CGS18

ACCESS THE MUSIC!
SCAN CODE WITH MOBILE APP
CANTATALEARNING.COM

TIPS TO SUPPORT LITERACY AT HOME

WHY READING AND SINGING WITH YOUR CHILD IS SO IMPORTANT

Daily reading with your child leads to increased academic achievement. Music and songs, specifically rhyming songs, are a fun and easy way to build early literacy and language development. Music skills correlate significantly with both phonological awareness and reading development. Singing helps build vocabulary and speech development. And reading and appreciating music together is a wonderful way to strengthen your relationship.

READ AND SING EVERY DAY!

TIPS FOR USING CANTATA LEARNING BOOKS AND SONGS DURING YOUR DAILY STORY TIME

1. As you sing and read, point out the different words on the page that rhyme. Suggest other words that rhyme.

2. Memorize simple rhymes such as Itsy Bitsy Spider and sing them together. This encourages comprehension skills and early literacy skills.

3. Use the questions in the back of each book to guide your singing and storytelling.

4. Read the included sheet music with your child while you listen to the song. How do the music notes correlate to the words of the song?

5. Sing along on the go and at home. Access music by scanning the QR code on each Cantata book, or by using the included CD. You can also stream or download the music for free to your computer, smartphone, or mobile device.

Devoting time to daily reading shows that you are available for your child. Together, you are building language, literacy, and listening skills.

Have fun reading and singing!

Aesop was a storyteller who wrote hundreds of stories called **fables**. Each of these short tales taught a **moral**, or lesson. In this fable, a **milkmaid** carries home a pail full of milk. She is going to **churn** that milk into butter. She starts dreaming of all the things that will happen once she sells her butter. What lesson can be learned from the milkmaid and her pail?

Turn the page to find out.
Remember to sing along!

Oh, a milkmaid with her pail
was walking home one sunny day.

She had milk for churning butter
and was dreaming along the way.

She was dreaming of the butter
she would sell to buy some eggs.

From those eggs would hatch some chickens,
so she thought one sunny day.

She was dreaming of all her chickens
before they had even hatched.

But what if something happened
and down her bucket crashed?

Oh, the milkmaid with her pail
would sell the chicks to buy a **gown**.

All the people would smile at her
as she danced and twirled around.

As she danced and as she twirled
the milkmaid tripped over a stone.

And the milk pail that she carried
tipped and spilled across the road.

She was counting all her chickens before they had even hatched.

But what if something happened and down her bucket crashed?

17

Oh, the milkmaid with her pail spilled her milk upon the ground.

She would not get any butter, any chickens, or a gown.

She had counted all her chickens
before they had even hatched.

But then something happened
and all her dreams were smashed.

So the moral of our story:
wait until your plans have hatched,
or something else could happen
and your dreams will all be smashed.

SONG LYRICS
The Milkmaid and Her Pail

Oh, a milkmaid with her pail
was walking home one sunny day.
She had milk for churning butter
and was dreaming along the way.

She was dreaming of the butter
she would sell to buy some eggs.
From those eggs would hatch some
    chickens,
so she thought one sunny day.

She was dreaming of all her chickens
before they had even hatched.
But what if something happened
and down her bucket crashed?

Oh, the milkmaid with her pail
would sell the chicks to buy a gown.
All the people would smile at her
as she danced and twirled around.

As she danced and as she twirled
the milkmaid tripped over a stone.

And the milk pail that she carried
tipped and spilled across the road.

She was counting all her chickens
before they had even hatched.
But what if something happened
and down her bucket crashed?

Oh, the milkmaid with her pail
spilled her milk upon the ground.
She would not get any butter,
any chickens, or a gown.

She had counted all her chickens
before they had even hatched.
But then something happened
and all her dreams were smashed.

So the moral of our story:
wait until your plans have hatched,
or something else could happen
and your dreams will all be smashed.

The Milkmaid and Her Pail

Americana
Joseph Faison IV

Verse

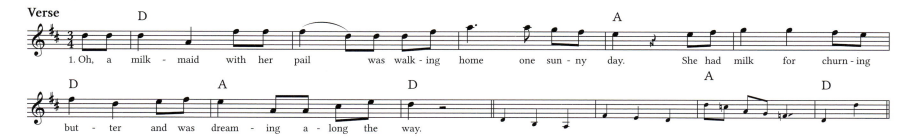

1. Oh, a milk - maid with her pail was walk - ing home one sun - ny day. She had milk for churn - ing but - ter and was dream - ing a - long the way.

Verse 2
She was dreaming of the butter
she would sell to buy some eggs.
From those eggs would hatch some chickens,
so she thought one sunny day.

Chorus

She was dream - ing of all her chick - ens be - fore they had e - ven hatched. But what if some - thing hap - pened and down her buck - et crashed?

Fine

Verse 3
Oh, the milkmaid with her pail
would sell the chicks to buy a gown.
All the people would smile at her
as she danced and twirled around.

Verse 4
As she danced and as she twirled
the milkmaid tripped over a stone.
And the milk pail that she carried
tipped and spilled across the road.

Chorus
She was counting all her chickens
before they had even hatched.
But what if something happened
and down her bucket crashed?

Verse 5
Oh, the milkmaid with her pail
spilled her milk upon the ground.
She would not get any butter,
any chickens, or a gown.

Chorus
She had counted all her chickens
before they had even hatched.
But then something happened
and all her dreams were smashed.
(no interlude)

Chorus
So the moral of our story:
wait until your plans have hatched,
or something else could happen
and your dreams will all be smashed.

GLOSSARY

Aesop—a legendary storyteller who is said to have lived in ancient Greece around 600 BCE

churn—to stir milk until it becomes butter

gown—a dress

fables—short stories that often have animal characters and teach a lesson

milkmaid—an old-fashioned term for woman who makes milk into cream, butter, and cheese

moral—a lesson often found in a story

GUIDED READING ACTIVITIES

1. What does it mean when someone says, "Don't count your chickens before they hatch"?

2. Did you ever get excited about going somewhere or getting something, only to have your dreams dashed? How did it make you feel? Is there something you could have done differently?

3. Is there something you dream of doing or having? What are some small steps you could take to get the thing you want? Draw a picture of them.

TO LEARN MORE

Berendes, Mary. *The Maid and the Milk Pail*. North Mankato, MN: Child's World, 2011.

Hoena, Blake. *Oh, My Darling, Clementine*. North Mankato, MN: Cantata Learning, 2016.

Hoena, Blake. *The Ant and the Grasshopper*. North Mankato, MN: Cantata Learning, 2018.

Taus-Bolstad, Stacy. *From Grass to Milk*. Minneapolis: Lerner, 2013.